MARVEL STUDIOS

THOR
THE MIGHTY AVENGER

READ-ALONG
STORYBOOK AND CD

This is the story of how Thor, the son of King Odin of Asgard, was cast away to Earth, where he became one of the realm's finest defenders. You can read along with me in your book. You will know it is time to turn the page when you hear this sound. . . . Let's begin now.

marvelkids.com

Printed in the United States of America

First Edition, October 2016
1 3 5 7 9 10 8 6 4 2
Library of Congress Control Number: 2016901988
ISBN 978-1-4847-8173-9
FAC-008598-16232

It was the day of the coronation of a new king of Asgard, the mightiest of the Nine Realms of the cosmos. All of Asgard was gathered in the throne room. For centuries, the mighty Odin All-Father had defended Asgard, Earth, and the other realms from destruction and had fought to keep peace in the universe. Now King Odin's eldest son, Thor, knelt before him to accept his father's crown.

From his throne, Odin looked down proudly on his son. "And on this day, I, Odin All-Father, proclaim you . . ."

Odin's voice trailed off. He could sense that there were intruders in the weapons vault. **"Frost Giants!"**

The Frost Giants hated the Asgardians. King Odin and his army had stopped the Frost Giants from taking over Earth, driving them back to their dark icy realm of Jotunheim. There, King Odin had defeated Laufey, the king of the Frost Giants, and taken the source of their power, the Casket of Ancient Winters. Odin kept the Casket of Ancient Winters heavily guarded in Asgard so that it would never fall back into the hands of the Jotuns.

King Odin, Thor, and Loki, Odin's youngest son, went to the vault to investigate. Three Frost Giants had broken in and tried to steal the Casket of Ancient Winters! Luckily, Odin's weapon, the Destroyer, had done its job and stopped the intruders. Odin was calm, but Thor was furious.

"The Jotuns must pay for what they have done! They broke into the weapons vault. **I want to know *why*.**"

Thor wanted to attack the Frost Giants on Jotunheim, but King Odin refused. He was still the king and he didn't want to break the peace agreement between the Asgardians and the Frost Giants.

But Thor remained determined to confront the Frost Giants. He convinced his friends and Loki to accompany him to Jotunheim. Heimdall, the gatekeeper of Asgard, agreed to let them pass but warned them that he would not open the Bifröst, the bridge between realms, if their return threatened the safety of Asgard. Loki and Thor's friends looked worried. But Thor just shrugged it off. **"I have no plans to die today."**

On Jotunheim, Thor and his friends stood before Laufey, the king of the Frost Giants. When Thor asked him how the Frost Giants had forced their way into Asgard, Laufey warned of traitors in the house of King Odin. His words enraged Thor. "Do not dishonor my father's name with your lies!"

Laufey offered to let Thor and his friends leave without any consequences. Looking around at King Laufey's many guards, Loki tried to convince Thor to accept the offer and stand down. **"Thor, look around you. We're outnumbered."**

But as they turned to leave, King Laufey insulted Thor. Annoyed, Thor hurled his mighty hammer at Laufey, which drove the Frost Giants to attack the Asgardians! Together, the friends valiantly fought the Frost Giants, but King Laufey and his men trapped Thor and his friends at the edge of a cliff.

Suddenly, King Odin appeared from the sky on his horse. Thor was overjoyed.

"Father! We'll finish them together!"

But King Odin looked down on his son. "Silence!"

King Odin tried to convince King Laufey to maintain their peace agreement. "These are the actions of a boy. Treat them as such. You and I can end this here and now, before there's further bloodshed."

But King Laufey wanted to start a war.

Odin sighed. "So be it."

King Laufey raised his frosty dagger to attack King Odin. But with a burst of light, King Odin transported himself, Loki, Thor, and their friends back to Asgard.

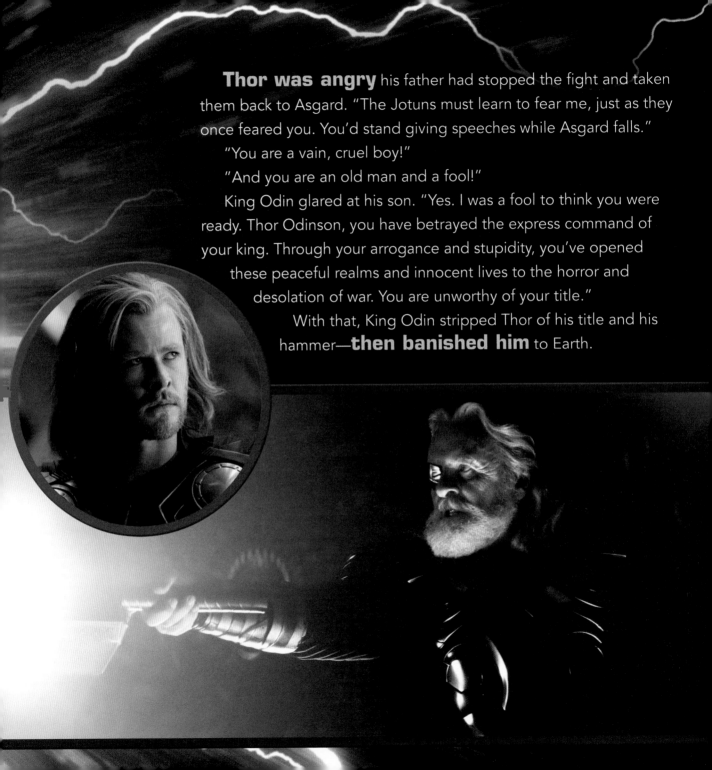

Thor was angry his father had stopped the fight and taken them back to Asgard. "The Jotuns must learn to fear me, just as they once feared you. You'd stand giving speeches while Asgard falls."

"You are a vain, cruel boy!"

"And you are an old man and a fool!"

King Odin glared at his son. "Yes. I was a fool to think you were ready. Thor Odinson, you have betrayed the express command of your king. Through your arrogance and stupidity, you've opened these peaceful realms and innocent lives to the horror and desolation of war. You are unworthy of your title."

With that, King Odin stripped Thor of his title and his hammer—**then banished him** to Earth.

On Earth, Thor crashed into an SUV chasing a magnetic storm. The driver, an astrophysicist named Jane Foster, jumped out to see if he was hurt.

"Do me a favor and don't be dead."

Thor was dazed but uninjured. Still, Jane and her colleagues Erik Selvig and Darcy Lewis dropped Thor off at the hospital to get checked out. Thor, not understanding that the doctors were trying to help him, **pushed them away**.

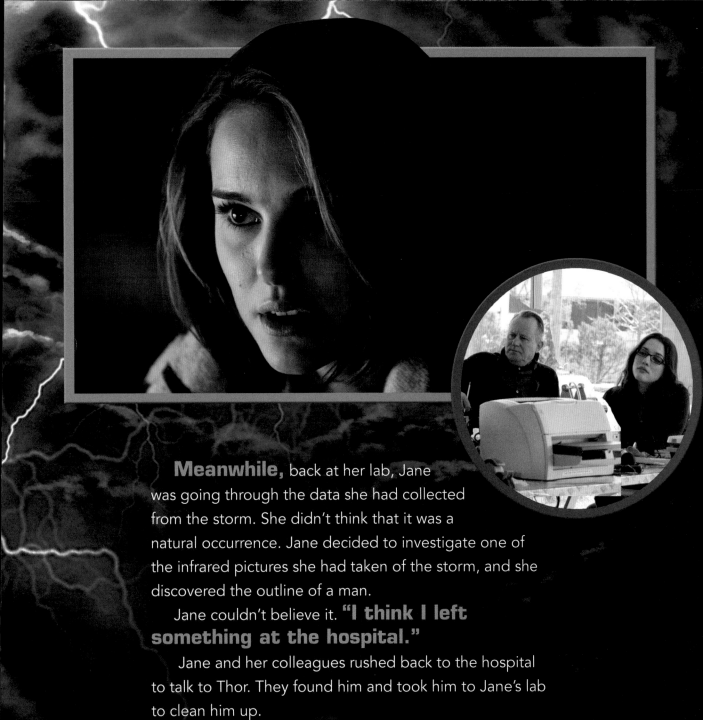

Meanwhile, back at her lab, Jane was going through the data she had collected from the storm. She didn't think that it was a natural occurrence. Jane decided to investigate one of the infrared pictures she had taken of the storm, and she discovered the outline of a man.

Jane couldn't believe it. **"I think I left something at the hospital."**

Jane and her colleagues rushed back to the hospital to talk to Thor. They found him and took him to Jane's lab to clean him up.

Back in Asgard, Loki was trying to figure something out. During the battle, one of the Frost Giants had touched his arm, turning it blue when it should have burned him. Loki went down to the vault looking for answers and picked up the Casket of Ancient Winters. When he turned around, his skin was glowing blue once again and **King Odin was standing behind him**.

Loki looked at his father. "The casket wasn't the only thing you took from Jotunheim that day, was it?"

King Odin shook his head. After the battle on Jotunheim, he had stumbled upon a newborn in the temple and taken him back to Asgard. That baby was Loki, son of King Laufey. "You were an innocent child. I thought we could unite our kingdoms one day. Bring about an alliance. Bring about permanent peace through you. But those plans no longer matter."

Loki was enraged. "It all makes sense now why you favored Thor all these years. Because no matter how much you claimed to love me, you could never have a Frost Giant sitting on the throne of Asgard."

Odin suddenly clutched his chest, collapsing on the stairs. He had fallen into the Odinsleep, and **there was no telling when he would wake**.

Back on Earth, Jane, Selvig, and Darcy were at a diner with Thor. Jane was trying to get answers out of him when they overheard some patrons talking about a satellite crash in the desert. No one could pull the satellite out of the ground, and the government had come in to claim it. Thor immediately stood up and asked where the satellite was. Then he walked out of the diner, toward the site.

Jane ran after him. "Where are you going?"

Thor kept walking. "**To get what belongs to me.** It's not what they say it is." He knew that object was actually his mighty hammer, Mjölnir. "If you take me there now, I'll tell you everything you wish to know."

But Selvig didn't trust Thor and warned Jane that he was dangerous and delusional. They said good-bye to Thor as he kept walking to find his hammer.

But when Jane returned to her lab, it was being ransacked. The man in charge was Agent Coulson of S.H.I.E.L.D. Coulson and his men were confiscating all of Jane's research and equipment!

Coulson offered Jane a check, which she threw to the ground. "**This is my life!** I can't just buy replacements at Radio Shack. I made most of this equipment myself. I'm on the verge of understanding something extraordinary. And everything I know about this phenomenon is either in this lab or in this book, and you can't just take this awa—Hey!"

Coulson smiled politely, then grabbed Jane's notebook out of her hand and drove away. A little later, Jane, Darcy, and Selvig sat on the roof, trying to figure out their next move.

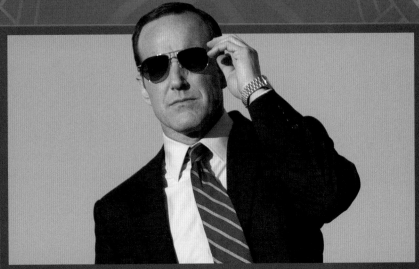

In Asgard, Thor's friends decided to ask King Odin to reconsider Thor's banishment, but instead of their king, they found Loki sitting on the throne, wearing his ceremonial helmet.

Loki smiled down on them. "Father has fallen into the Odinsleep. Mother fears he may never awaken again. You can bring your urgent matter to me . . . your king."

Reluctantly, Thor's friends bowed before Loki and asked him to allow Thor to come home. But Loki refused. **"My first command cannot be to undo the All-Father's last."**

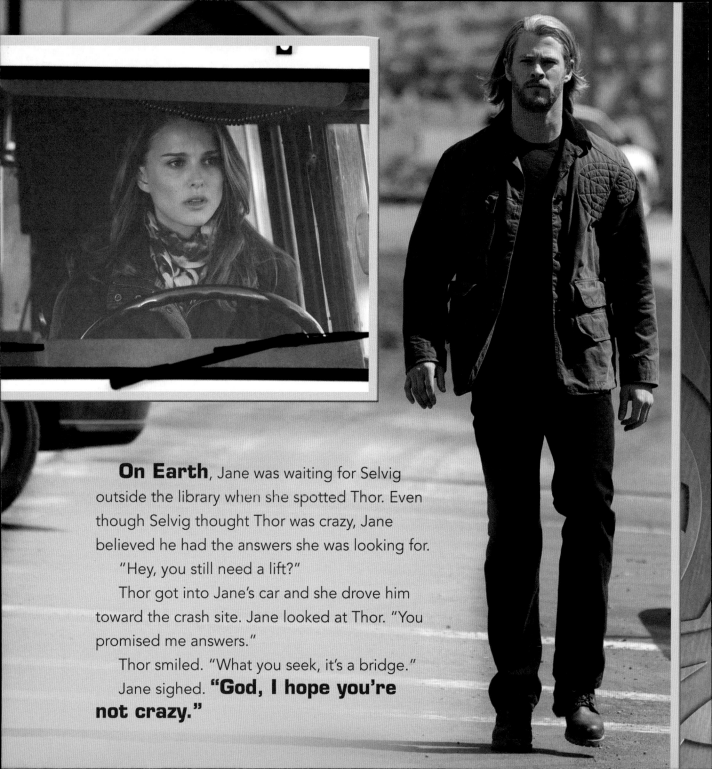

On Earth, Jane was waiting for Selvig outside the library when she spotted Thor. Even though Selvig thought Thor was crazy, Jane believed he had the answers she was looking for.

"Hey, you still need a lift?"

Thor got into Jane's car and she drove him toward the crash site. Jane looked at Thor. "You promised me answers."

Thor smiled. "What you seek, it's a bridge."

Jane sighed. **"God, I hope you're not crazy."**

When Jane and Thor reached the crash site, there was a makeshift fortress surrounded by armed guards. Jane was surprised. "That's no satellite crash. They would have hauled the wreckage away; they wouldn't have built a city around it."

Thor told Jane he was going in to get their things. Jane looked at Thor skeptically. "No, look what's down there. You think you're just gonna walk in, grab our stuff, and walk out?"

Thor grinned. **"No. I'm gonna fly out."**

Moving quickly, Thor made his way into the fortress and knocked past the armed guards. He fought them off easily even without his superhuman strength. Then he saw his hammer stuck in the ground in the middle of the fortress. Grinning, Thor gripped the hammer's handle tightly and pulled as Agent Coulson watched. But Thor could not pick up the hammer! It remained stuck in the ground. He roared angrily at the sky and fell to his knees. Odin had placed a spell on the hammer. **Only one who was truly worthy of its power could wield it.**

With Thor distracted by his failure, Agent Coulson's men quickly moved in. They handcuffed Thor and dragged him away.

Agent Coulson started questioning Thor. Coulson believed Thor was a spy, so he wanted to know where Thor was trained and who he worked for. But Thor wouldn't answer his questions.

Coulson left the room to take a call. Suddenly, Loki appeared in front of Thor. He came bearing bad news. "Father is dead. Your banishment, the threat of a new war, it was too much for him to bear. The burden of the throne has fallen to me now."

Thor couldn't believe it. He asked Loki if he could return home. But Loki shook his head. "The truce with Jotunheim is conditional upon your exile. And Mother has forbidden your return. This is good-bye, Brother."

Thor hung his head, holding back tears. "I am sorry."

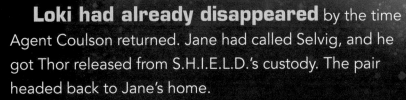

Loki had already disappeared by the time Agent Coulson returned. Jane had called Selvig, and he got Thor released from S.H.I.E.L.D.'s custody. The pair headed back to Jane's home.

On Jane's rooftop, Thor explained the Nine Realms to her, drawing a picture. "Your world is one of the Nine Realms of the cosmos, linked to each other by the branches of Yggdrasil, the World's Tree. Now you see it every day without realizing, the images glimpsed through . . . what did you call it . . . this Hubble telescope."

Jane listened, fascinated, as Thor described the other realms to her, including Asgard. **She was beginning to care for Thor.**

Meanwhile, Loki traveled to Jotunheim. He revealed to Laufey that he had let the three Frost Giants into Asgard to ruin Thor's coronation day, and he also made an offer to the king of the Frost Giants.

"I will conceal you and a handful of your soldiers, lead you into Odin's chambers, and you can slay him where he lies. Once Odin is dead, I will return the casket to you and you can return Jotunheim to all its . . . uh, glory."

Laufey accepted Loki's offer. But when Loki returned to Asgard, Heimdall was waiting at the gate with a suspicious gaze. He hadn't been able to see or hear Loki in Jotunheim.

Loki stared coldly at Heimdall. "You're sworn to obey me now. **You will open the Bifröst to no one.**"

In the palace of Asgard, Thor's friends were restless. They were trying to find a way to help Thor get back home when Heimdall summoned them. Since Heimdall was bound by his command to the king, he could not open the Bifröst, but **Thor's friends could**! As Heimdall turned his back and walked away, Thor's friends opened the bridge to Earth. They landed on Earth and wandered through the small town until they finally found Thor at Jane's lab.

Thor was glad to see his friends, but he told them to return to Asgard. "You should not have come. You know I cannot go home. My father is dead because of me. I must remain in exile."

His friends looked at him, confused. They told Thor his father was still alive. Loki had lied to him!

But Loki had observed Thor's friends leaving Asgard. Annoyed, he traveled down to the vault and freed the Destroyer, commanding it to get rid of Thor. "Ensure my brother does not return. **Destroy everything!**"

After that, Loki confronted Heimdall at the gates. "For your act of treason, you are relieved of your duties as gatekeeper and no longer citizen of Asgard."

Heimdall drew his sword to fight Loki, but Loki swiftly pulled out the Casket of Ancient Winters and froze Heimdall in a block of ice. Using the Bifröst, Loki sent the Destroyer down to Earth. The machine saw Coulson's S.H.I.E.L.D. agents at the hammer site. **It began blasting the agents and everything in its path!**

Thor and his friends saw the Destroyer as it approached Earth and headed toward the town. The Asgardians wanted to fight the Destroyer. But without his hammer, Thor was just a man. "I can help get these people to safety. We'll need some time."

Thor's friends agreed to distract the Destroyer while Thor and Jane evacuated the town. The Asgardians battled the Destroyer, but it was too powerful. Thor raced over to his friends. "You must return to Asgard. **You have to stop Loki.**"

His friends didn't want to leave without him, but Thor had a plan.

Leaving his friends and Jane behind, Thor walked toward the giant machine.

Thor looked up at the Destroyer. He knew that Loki could hear him on Asgard. "Brother, whatever I have done to wrong you, whatever I have done to lead you to do this, I am truly sorry. But these people are innocent. Taking their lives will gain you nothing. So take mine and end this."

The Destroyer backhanded Thor, sending him reeling. **Thor was knocked out.**

As the Destroyer turned away, Thor's hammer released itself from the ground and rocketed through the air toward Thor.

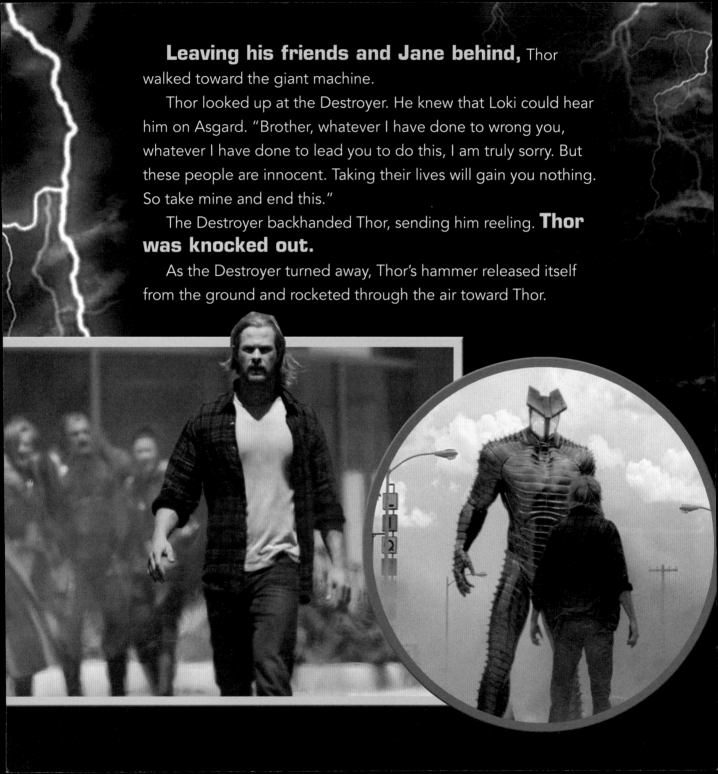

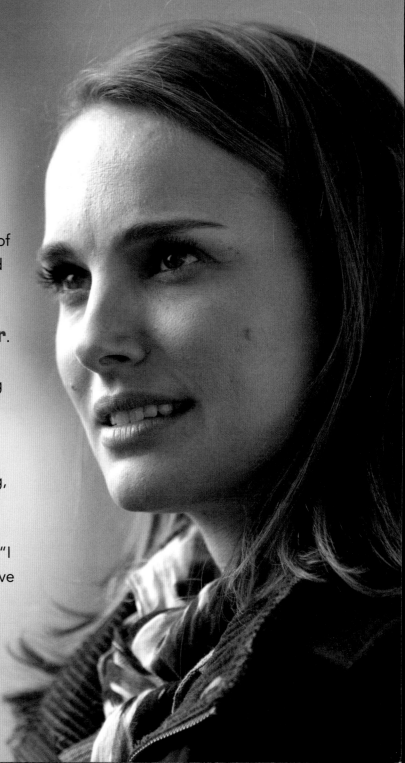

Thor's selfless act to defend Jane and the townspeople had made him worthy of the hammer! In a bolt of lightning, Thor's powers returned to him. Using Mjölnir, Thor summoned a mighty storm and defeated the Destroyer. But he still needed to get back to Asgard to stop Loki. Grabbing Jane, Thor flew to the Bifröst site, where he called for the gatekeeper to open the bridge.

Hearing the call of a true king, Heimdall broke through the ice and opened the gate.

Thor said good-bye to Jane. "I must go back to Asgard. But I give you my word. I will return for you."

In Asgard, Loki had already let Laufey and his soldiers into the palace to kill King Odin. As Laufey knelt over the sleeping Odin, Loki blasted the Frost Giant king with his scepter, destroying him for good. "Your death came by the son of Odin."

As the queen hugged Loki, Thor appeared. "Loki. Why don't you tell her how you sent the Destroyer to kill our friends? To kill me?"

Loki grinned wickedly. "It's good to have you back. Now if you'll excuse me, I have to destroy Jotunheim." With that, a blast from Loki's scepter sent Thor hurtling through a wall.

Loki raced to the gates and opened the Bifröst to Jotunheim. Using the Casket of Ancient Winters, he blasted the Bifröst with its power, and its energy began destroying the icy realm. Desperately, Thor tried to stop it with his hammer, but it was no use. He turned to his brother. "Why have you done this?"

Loki sneered at Thor. "To prove to Father that I am the worthy son. When he wakes, I will have destroyed that race of monsters, **and I will be true heir to the throne**."

The two brothers flew toward each other. Thor trapped Loki and began to hit the Rainbow Bridge with his hammer. Before he brought down his hammer for the final blow, he paused. "Forgive me, Jane." Both brothers tumbled over the edge into space as the portal exploded and were caught by King Odin, who had awoken from the Odinsleep. But Loki let go of his father's spear and fell into space.

With Asgard and Earth both safe and Jotunheim preserved, Thor was finally able to mourn the loss of his brother, as well as his dear friend Jane. He remained hopeful that one day he would find a way to reconnect the Bifröst with Earth again and reunite with Jane. But Thor also had something to be glad about. His father, King Odin, was alive and well.

King Odin was proud of Thor. **"You'll be a wise king."**

Thor smiled. "I have much to learn. I know that now."